MAKE ME A WORLD is an imprint dedicated to exploring the vast possibilities of contemporary childhood. We strive to imagine a universe in which no young person is invisible, in which no kid's story is erased, in which no glass ceiling presses down on the dreams of a child. Then we publish books for that world, where kids ask hard questions and we struggle with them together, where dreams stretch from eons ago into the future and we do our best to provide road maps to where these young folks want to be. We make books where the children of today can see themselves and each other. When presented with fences, with borders, with limits, with all the kinds of chains that hobble imaginations and hearts, we proudly say—no.

Visit us on the Web! rhcbooks.com
Educators and librarians, for a variety of teaching tools, visit us at RHTeachersLibrarians.com

Library of Congress Cataloging-in-Publication Data is available upon request.
ISBN 978-1-5247-1754-4 (hardcover)
ISBN 978-1-5247-1755-1 (lib. bdg.)
ISBN 978-1-5247-1756-8 (ebook)

The text of this book is set in Cochin LT Pro.
The artist used colored pencil on paper to create the illustrations for this book.
Book design by Martha Rago

MANUFACTURED IN CHINA
March 2020
10 9 8 7 6 5 4 3 2 1
First Edition

RAY JAYAWARDHANA

Child of the Universe

Illustrated by

RAUL COLÓN

MAKE ME A WORLD

New York

To Nehara and Tehan,
who light up my little corner of the universe
–R.J.

For Rachel, a star mother herself
–R.C.

My father says I am made of stars.
He turns off the light so it is dark.

We look at the moon from the edge of my bed.
"The universe conspired to make you," he said.

Just like the sun gives shine to the moon,
you light up the world beyond this room.

Like the majesty of the Milky Way's grace,
your curly hair swirls over your face.

There are galaxies in your smile so wide.
The cosmos is reflected in the depths of your eyes.

Like faraway planets only telescopes can see,
with hills and valleys, glaciers and seas . . .

. . . you are grand and marvelous, strong and mysterious.

The history of the world is in your fingertips.

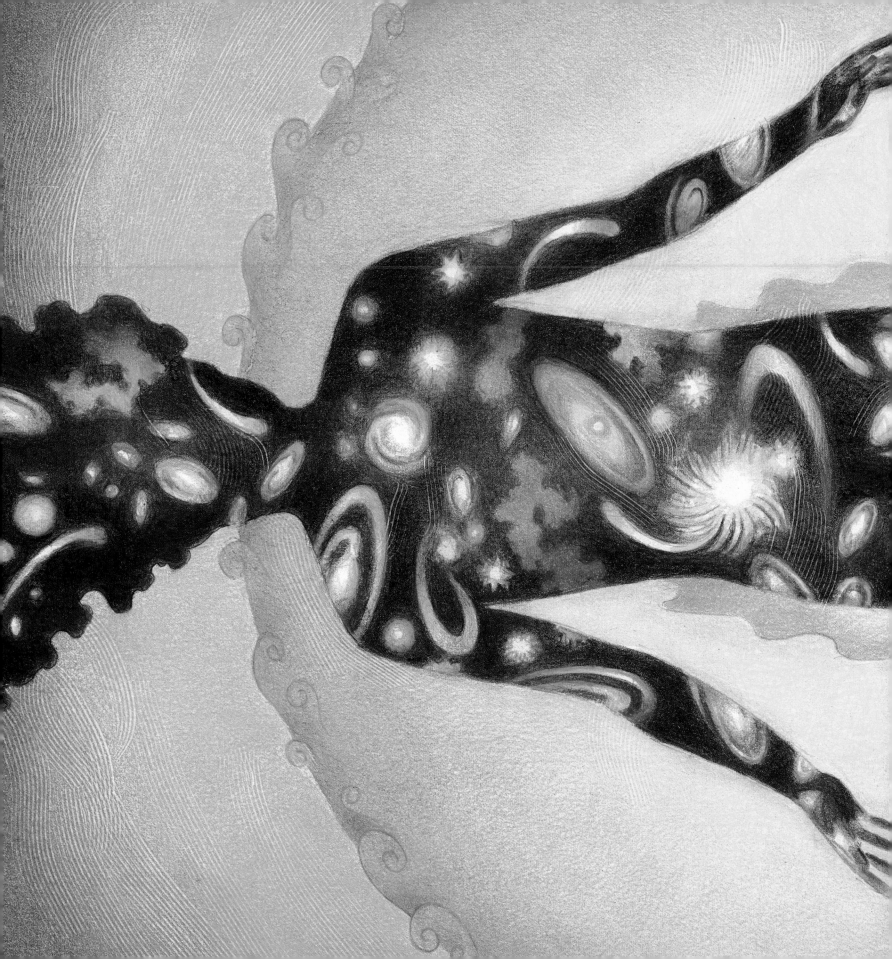

The iron in your blood, the calcium in your bones,
are made up of stars that lived long ago.

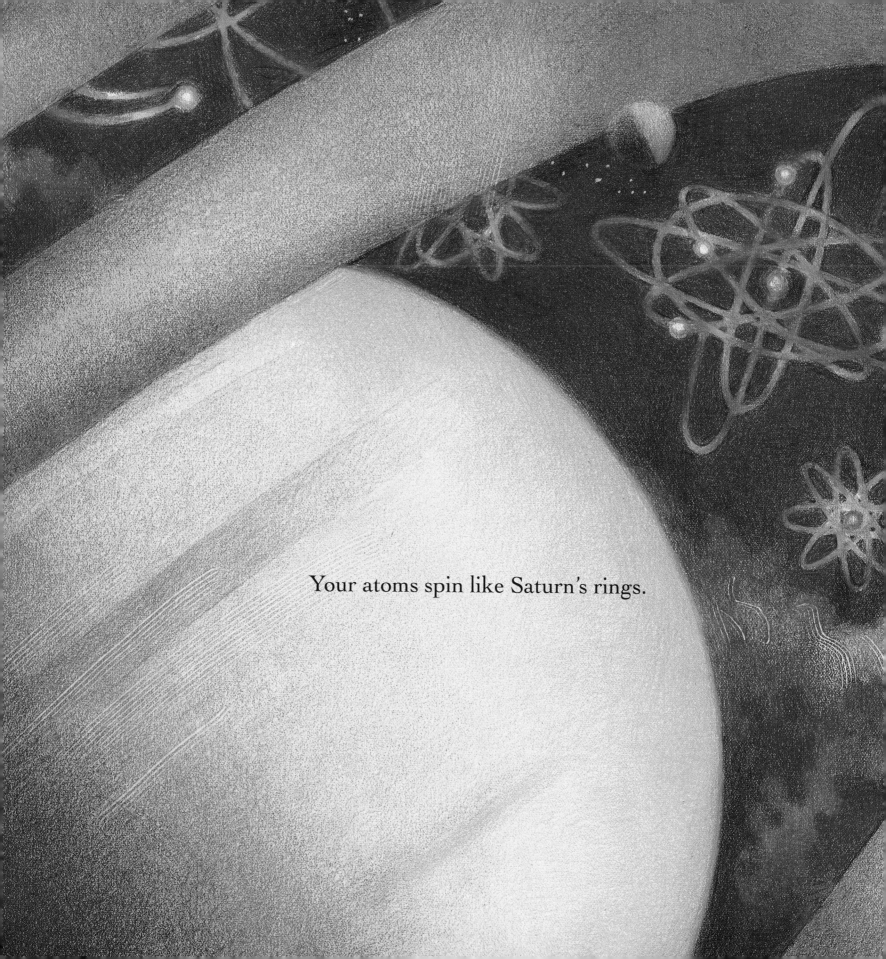

Your atoms spin like Saturn's rings.

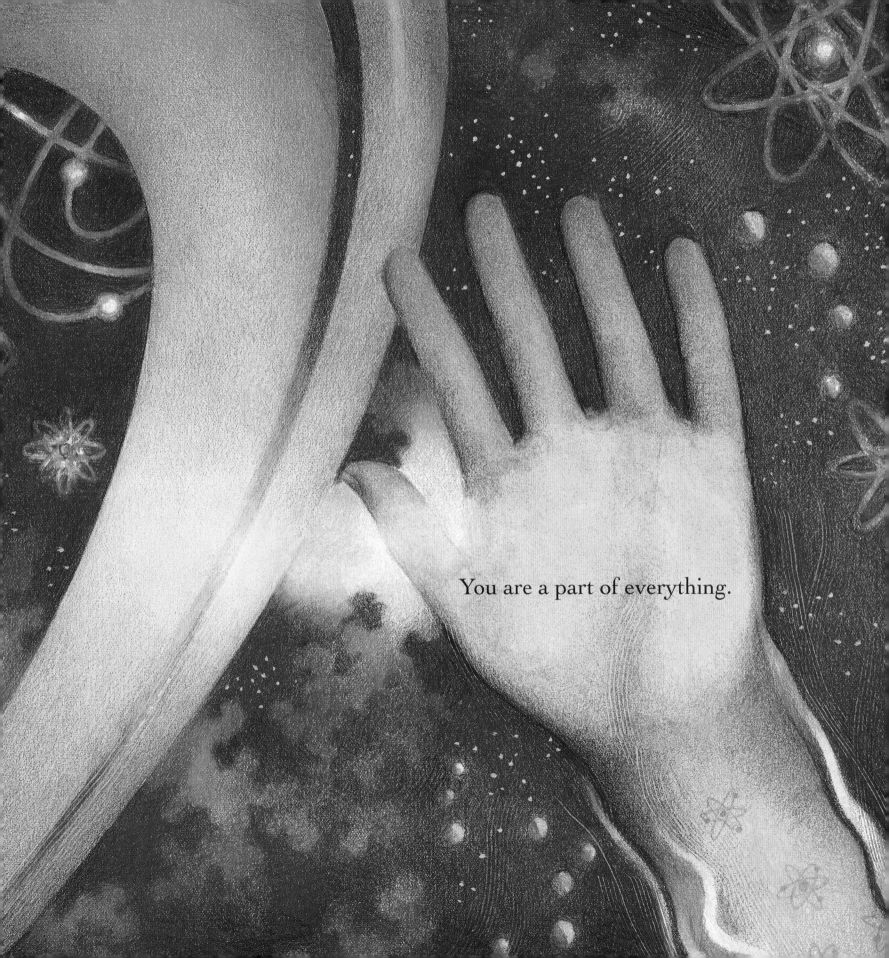

You are a part of everything.

Of constellations and arctic ice,
of waves that move at the speed of light.

Of starbursts brighter than fireworks,
you are a child of the universe.

"Now get under the covers," my father says.
"It's time for you to go to bed."

He tucks me in and through the window I see
the great, full moon smiling back at me.

I close my eyes and tonight I'll dream
of stardust and planets and all that's between.

AUTHOR'S NOTE

Amid the comforts and distractions of modern life, the cosmos may appear remote, untouchable, and irrelevant, especially to those of us who inhabit cities, where bright lights swamp the true splendor of the night sky. We might think of the universe as being "out there," disconnected from our daily realities and pressing concerns here on Earth.

But that's simply not the case. It is only a thin sliver of air that separates us from the rest of the cosmos. We are connected to the universe at large, and are influenced by it, in countless and intimate ways.

For one, as Joni Mitchell sang nearly fifty years ago, "We are stardust." The calcium in our bones, the iron in our blood, and the oxygen we breathe come from ancient stars that lived and died before our own sun was born. In fact, almost all the elements in the periodic table were cooked up through nuclear reactions inside stars.

For another, growing evidence suggests that some molecules relevant for life were forged in the space between the stars. A good fraction of the water in our oceans—and in our bodies—may be older than Earth, having assembled in the chilly depths of the gas cloud that spawned our solar system. Astronomers have discovered a variety of complex, carbon-bearing molecules in distant stellar nurseries. Put simply, there is no escaping the fact that the universe is in our DNA: stars made the stuff of life; meteorites delivered water and organic molecules forged in interstellar space to the young Earth; lunar tides and comet impacts shaped evolution. New findings from astronomy, geology, and biology reveal the surprising extent to which cosmic processes have affected the origin and development of life on our planet.

Even today, we are not immune to the whims of the cosmos: umpteen particles from space bombard Earth day and night; asteroid collisions pose a small but serious risk to our very existence; giant solar flares not only produce spectacular auroras but also disrupt satellites, air travel, and power grids, making our technological society vulnerable to "space weather."

Our cosmic connections go well beyond the physical, of course. For thousands of years, people feared, revered, and even relied upon the heavens above: comets were seen as omens of death and destruction; temples were often aligned with the passage of the sun, moon, or planets; and the stars helped keep track of the harvesting seasons and served as valued beacons for navigation.

More recently, the universe has provided us with inspiration and fueled our imagination in numerous ways: photographs of Earthrise above the moon, taken by Apollo astronauts, called attention to the fragility of our world; violent outbursts on other stars have given us a new appreciation for the sun's beneficent nature; and the discovery of exoplanets by the thousands has brought questions of alien life and our cosmic solitude to the forefront.

Child of the Universe attempts to highlight these deep and enduring links—both physical and poetic—between the universe and us, and to nurture a sense of wonder about the great beyond.

BIBLIOGRAPHY

Jayawardhana, Ray. "Our Cosmic Selves." *The New York Times*, April 5, 2015.

"Q&A with Ray Jayawardhana." *GSAS Bulletin*. Harvard University, Fall 2014.

Sagan, Carl. *Cosmos*. New York: Random House, 1980.

This book was conceived during a Bogliasco Fellowship in Italy. The author wishes to thank the incomparable Christopher Myers for his central role in its development.

MAKE ME A WORLD

Somewhere, when it comes to science, we got lost. Perhaps it was when someone told you that if you weren't good at math, you couldn't be an astronaut. Or maybe you took a test, and it said you were more creative than logical. And maybe you looked at the children around you and thought you could see a budding artist in one particularly wild-eyed boy, and a perfect physicist in a particularly fastidious and orderly girl. You joke occasionally that you couldn't even add two and two.

What we have missed is that at the heart of great science, truly world-expanding research, there are dreams. Yes, every great scientist is first a dreamer. And more important than their ability to tabulate figures, or use the most advanced computer systems linked across the globe, is their ability to translate their dreams into stories that must be proven and tested.

Ray Jayawardhana is one such dreamer, an astronomer at the top of his field, who has literally discovered new worlds. Like all astronomers, he thinks of time in ways that could seem incredibly abstract to us. Words like "billions" and "light-years" flow through his vocabulary, almost like a song. He looks through telescopes on the tops of mountains in Hawaii and Chile, and he is looking back in time, at starlight that has outlasted the stars themselves. That night sky, sending messages from millions of years ago, is where his dreaming started, walking with his father in a moonlit garden in Sri Lanka when he was a boy.

And here in this book, he shares that dreaming with a new generation of dreamers, young people, like his daughter and son, who will know that all those billions of years, from the beginning of the universe until now, all that time and stardust, have come to a point, in the dreams of a child, paging through Raul Colón's pictures mirroring the cosmos, and Ray's text building a universe, big enough to hold all our dreams.

Christopher Myers